Mel the Chosen was illustrated with pencils
and inks and colored with watercolors.

Text, cover art, and interior illustrations copyright © 2021 by Rachele Aragno
Translation copyright © 2021 by Bao Dieci

All rights reserved. Published in the United States by RH Graphic, an imprint of
Random House Children's Books, a division of Penguin Random House LLC, New York.
Originally published as a hardcover in the Italian language in Italy by Bao Dieci, in 2020.

RH Graphic with the book design is a trademark of Penguin Random House LLC.

Visit us on the web and sign up for our newsletter! RHKidsGraphic.com • @RHKidsGraphic

Educators and librarians, for a variety of teaching tools, visit us at RHTeachersLibrarians.com

Library of Congress Cataloging-in-Publication Data is available upon request.
ISBN 978-0-593-30123-4 (pbk) — ISBN 978-0-593-30124-1 (hc)
ISBN 978-0-593-30125-8 (lib. bdg.) — ISBN 978-0-593-30126-5 (ebk)

Interior design and lettering by Patrick Crotty
Translation by Carla Roncalli Di Montorio

MANUFACTURED IN CHINA
10 9 8 7 6 5 4 3 2 1
First American Edition

A comic on every bookshelf.

# Rachele Aragno

MEL
the Chosen

We can't move again. . . .

I know, but what should I do? Give up my promotion?

Mel is growing up. She needs stability right now and . . .

And what?

THUMP

Isn't it too much of a change?

For my future! Yeah, right!

Nana and Grandpa would have said—

"Make your own decisions. Choose your own path."

MEOW

Huh?

MEOW

Hey, Octavius, stop!

MEOW

Get back here!

It all feels so pointless, like I don't have control over my own life.

Mom and Dad don't understand. They just do what they want. They don't care about what I think.

I'm not an object they can toss around wherever. If I were older, I'd tell them what's what.

Geez, thanks for the support. Some help you are!

MEOW

11

This is the Book of Return.

This can bring anything to life.

Wow . . .

That's what I thought, too, when I was a kid. I never thought I'd wake up like this!

Wake up? I'm still confused. Mr. Otto . . . who's Malcape?

You're the Chosen One—only you can contain such power.

Nothing's going to happen. Trust us.

I ...

The book will help you understand. Give the robin a stroke.

But it's ... dead.

Mel, please try. It's best to show you.

It was a Saturday morning, and I was cleaning my bike.

My dad and granddad had asked me . . .

. . . to go hunting with them.

It was odd to be invited, as I usually sabotaged their hunting trips.

They could be so cruel.

As soon as we got there, my father spotted a doe with her fawn.

The sheer thought of killing two at once was a real thrill for them.

I knew if I did anything . . .

. . . I'd be . . .

. . . punished.

But that would never stop me. So I chased the deer off.

Dad got very angry.

He told me I'd have to make my own way home.

I just wanted them to hear what I had to say.

Then something odd happened.

Withered as it was . . .

. . . the tree . . .

. . . suddenly filled with leaves.

Through the foliage . . .

. . . a kid popped out.

He understood my problem.

It's true! Adults will only listen to us if we get older. But I have a solution.

With this book you will bring all your granddad's hunting trophies back to life and that will make the adults listen! In exchange . . .

He kept on talking, but I had stopped listening. He mentioned growing up. To me, that meant freedom.

As soon as I got home, I took three stuffed animals from my father's study, and I tried.

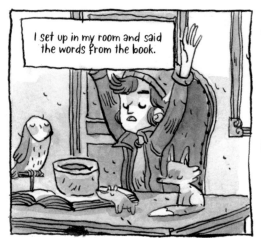

I set up in my room and said the words from the book.

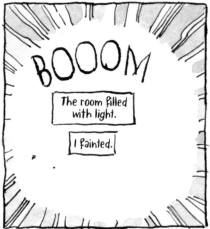

BOOOM

The room filled with light.

I fainted.

Otto! How lovely to see you again! Recognize me? I'm Malcape the Magnificent, King of Here&Now. I see my book was useful to you, so I am here to honor our agreement.

I hadn't realized that I had been tricked. In exchange for the book, we had sealed a pact.

He said that the only one who could break the pact was the Chosen One . . .

. . . and that I couldn't look for her. She would have to find me.

23

I had no idea of the trouble I would cause.

SNIF SNIF

MEOW

All these years I have been waiting for you. So when you came through the window . . .

You knew who I was!

SNIF

MEOW

MEOW

I don't understand why you'd want to be a kid again, but I'll help you. Let's find Malcape!

PRR PRRR

Oh, by the way . . . where does he live?

That's just the point, Mel, dear.

MEOW

Can I help you?

Hi, we just got here and . . .

ALVARO! WHERE ARE YOU?

. . . we are looking for . . .

I know—you're looking for a place.

Coming, honeypot.

Mr. Alvaro, there's been a misunderstanding. We are not looking for a place. . . .

Of course you are, just like everyone else.

Coming, sweetie pie!

Whatever it is you want, come on in and wait for me in the lounge!

ALVARO, COME NOW!

Who do you reckon "sweetie pie" is?

A friend, maybe?

Hey, a stuffed crow! You got the book?

Leave it alone. It's for the best.

But, Otto . . .

Poor crow . . .

OH! THIS MUST BE SWEETIE PIE!

36

Hello, dear, my name is Carlotta.

Mel. Nice to meet you.

I'm Otto.

I'm not talking to you!

I can see you're worried.

Carlotta... we are looking for this guy.

UMPH

He's called Malcape. He tricked my friend Otto and took something very important from him. Can you help us?

38

I worked at the palace for a long time, but... that's a whole other story. I can be your guide through the entire kingdom.

I have a very detailed map if you need it.

METAPHYSICAL SWAMPS

We can explore beyond the queen's palace, wherever you wish to go!

We just want to find Malcape. Where does he live?

In the metaphysical Swamps, quite a ways from here.

No one has ever had the courage to challenge him.

There's a first time for everything. Mel will do it.

I don't doubt that.

Keep in mind that the cost of making a wish come true isn't always worth it.

Thank you for your help.

Good luck.

Say hi to the queen for us!

Will do, Carlotta!

Be careful what you wish for, Mel. Malcape might make it come true.

That's because you're a kid who doesn't know anything beyond what she sees.

TSK!

Wait here, please. I shall announce you to the queen.

NO ENTRY FOR CHILDREN, BABOONS, OR HATLESS ADULTS!

The queen lets us into the palace, and you're still sulking? That's childish.

No, it's not! Who cares about the giant room? The queen is a bully who is holding her own mother prisoner!

These are very harsh accusations.

The queen would never do that. You're a liar!

And you're nothing but a silly crow who has been deceived!

I KNOW WHAT I SAW!

Dinner is served. The queen is expecting you.

We will continue this conversation later.

Ladies and gentlemen, it is our privilege to have you. Your Majesty, this is Mr. Otto, miss Mel, and—

My darling! Looking as stunning as ever.

Mel, I would like to thank you with this gift.

A perfume that returns you to how you are meant to be.

FSSSSS

Look after yourselves, and be careful!

FSSSSSS

You were right about the queen.

I should have listened to you both. I'm sorry.

63

Don't apologize, Mel.

I'm the one who is sorry. We shouldn't have dismissed your concerns the way we did.

I'm used to it. Nobody ever listens to kids.

That's why I can't wait to grow up!

Don't joke about that! It's not something you should wish for!

All right, grouchy. Hey, what's down there?

Malcape searched every inch of the river but never found it.

Only you can find this charm.

...

GULP

There's no instruction manual, but one thing's for certain, Mel. You . . .

. . . are the only one who can activate the charm and make it work!

Me? I didn't even know it existed!

This is for you. Stay with us for the night!

Thanks! But I'm . . .

Oh! Pj's! They're cute!

It's late, so we can stay if you want.

THANKS

Tell us a story, Mel!

Oh, I have a good one. This is the story of a boy named Otto. One morning he was—

Have you forgotten why you hated being a kid so much?

No, I haven't, but . . .

Well, now you're an adult who still doesn't listen!

Uh . . . hi!

What are you doing in there?

I'm locked in.

I was sad and ended up crying so much I made a lake out of my tears.

101

I was walking along the River of Life, and I felt vibrations in the air, like something was calling me.

It's the lost charm those children were telling us about!

It's as though it knew me. I don't know how to explain. . . .

So shiny!

How can that be?

They must have recognized Mel as the Chosen One.

I have an idea!

Could you take us to the Swamps?

*We've been waiting for this moment for so long!

*Now that Mel is here, Malcape will get his due!
**The girl seems strong and driven. I'm sure she'll succeed!
***I sure hope so! I oh-so-miss being a guardian!

TUMP

TUMP

TUMP

Here we are. The metaphysical Swamps.

139

144

Every day your parents and friends have done nothing but stifle you and try to control you.

No—

Behind this door you will find a new life, a world in which you make all your own choices. In a nutshell . . .

Freedom.

I don't believe you!

Still, what do you want from me? What can you achieve from making my wish come true?

Your charm will do as I say.

How can that be? What do you need it for?

Your charm is a key. It can open doors between kingdoms and worlds that you can't even imagine. Think of all the wishes I could grant in all those places. Nobody will be able to stop me, ever.

I made a mistake!
I can't let him do this.
I have to go back and
hide the charm.

TUMP

TUMP

I can't let him leave. I have to close the door!

He's too strong!

All thanks to you!

What did Malcape want with you? How did you beat him?

179

# AUTHOR'S NOTE

*Mel the Chosen* is a very special and deeply emotional project for me. I had been carrying this idea with me for my entire life and am finally able to share it with the world. At the heart of the story are the fears of a little girl, as told by her adult counterpart. Ideally, Melvina will return for more adventures—maybe even as a teenager and then as an adult. Thank you, readers, for cheering on Mel on her journey to grow up—without being in a hurry to do so.

# HOW HERE&NOW WAS BORN

*or*

## How Melvina Falls into Otto's Window

I was thirteen when my grandfather passed away; he was like a second father to me. Up until that moment, my childhood had been perfect: a little bubble left untouched by the outside world. For the first time I realized that even in my little nest horrible things could happen—that there were unknown monsters capable of hurting me. It was a delicate moment. Adolescence is a whirlwind of fluctuating emotions that seem unmanageable, and this fracture that I felt inside only made things worse. But one night, Melvina, my alter ego, arrived. She, too, had a lot of problems and did not feel understood, she had lost her grandparents, and she wanted to grow up and escape from the adolescent years that seemed like a burden too heavy for her shoulders. I quickly drew her. Over time I have changed her dress, height, and age, but her rebellious red hair remains unchanged and distinguishes her from the crowd. My teenage self realized that Melvina could do things that were impossible for me, such as traveling to other worlds or managing unlimited ports.

Thus was born Here&Now, a colorful place full of weird characters who do weird things. Here&Now also became the new home of Melvina's grandparents, who are not dead but have just moved there due to circumstances. Here&Now is a new world for Melvina, made up of happy thoughts and incredible adventures that allow her to explore it far and wide. How does she get there? By meeting Otto, an unlikely but very special friend whom she gets to know by falling through a dormer window into his room. (My childhood bedroom was in an attic, and I learned to love roofs!) I grew up while writing this story, and in doing so, I met other monsters, perhaps even scarier than I ever realized they could be. I decided to let Melvina meet a version of one of those monsters so that she could help me defeat it with her power. Malcape, with his long claws, entered the scene about ten years later. This ruthless antagonist allowed me to expand the world of Here&Now, to make Melvina's power grow, and to make her even stronger. By giving Melvina an amulet, I strengthened my own ability to face adversity. Melvina's story began many years ago, and like me, it was immature and angry. In the course of making this book, Melvina grew in awareness and intensity. She and I have been through a lot (and we will go through even more), but now we have our power and our special world.

The children of the cemetery
(They are all wearing pajamas.)

# THE MAGIC ITEMS

### THE BOOK OF RETURN

This book was created by the Supreme Wizards and brings creatures from any world back to life by transforming them into anthropomorphic beings. It should be used with great caution.

## THE TRANSPORT KEY

The key is used to transport someone to places that are dangerous or too abstract for their body. Its origins are lost in the mists of time.

## THE AMULET OF THE CHOICE

The amulet was born from the sacrifice of a bee in love with Melvina. It had never happened before, and for this reason nobody really knows its power. The amulet only works in contact with Mel, the Chosen One.

# THE MAP OF HERE&NOW

The map was created by the cartographer Leompiade de' Sac, an elderly scholar who lives at the court. He created all the maps of the Here&Now universe. It is said that you can reach any place on the map simply by touching it.

# THE PERFUME OF THE QUEEN

It is a magical perfume created by Soffimiellini Mice. It is used to change the height of those who wear it.

# THE SCEPTER OF CREEPING, HISSING LORDS

The scepter belongs to Malcape and the creeping ones. Skilled shape-shifters, they have always stood out for their cruelty and thirst for power. They are known as the Three S.

## HAPPY THOUGHTS

Happy Thoughts are made up of emotions and are released from the minds of the inhabitants of Here&Now as they are formed. They can be used as a light source in homes or streets as they flood the room with positive feelings.

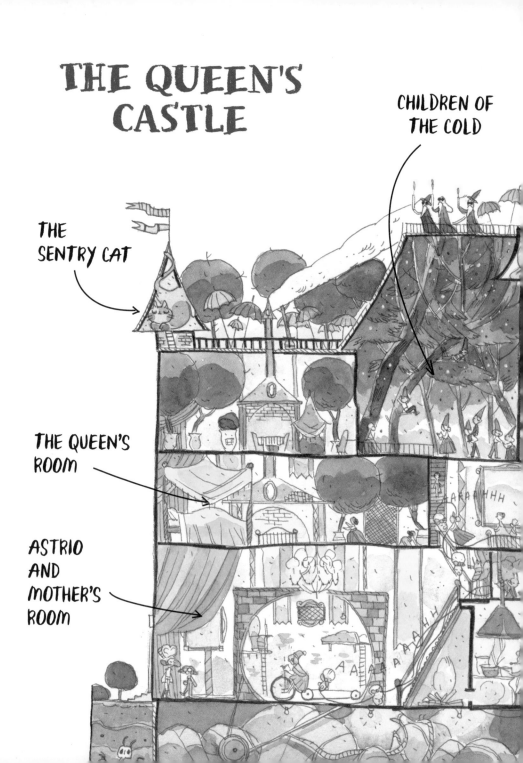

# THE QUEEN'S CASTLE

CHILDREN OF THE COLD

THE SENTRY CAT

THE QUEEN'S ROOM

ASTRIO AND MOTHER'S ROOM

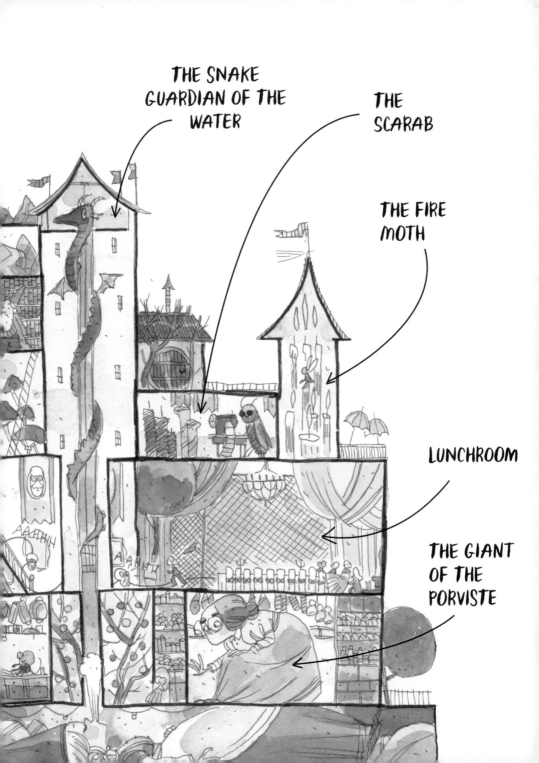

THE SNAKE
GUARDIAN OF THE
WATER

THE
SCARAB

THE FIRE
MOTH

LUNCHROOM

THE GIANT
OF THE
PORVISTE

# FIND YOUR VOICE
## WITH ONE OF THESE EXCITING GRAPHIC NOVELS

## PRESENTED BY RH GRAPHIC

### @RHKIDSGRAPHIC

## A GRAPHIC NOVEL ON EVERY BOOKSHELF